Fly-in to the Boonies

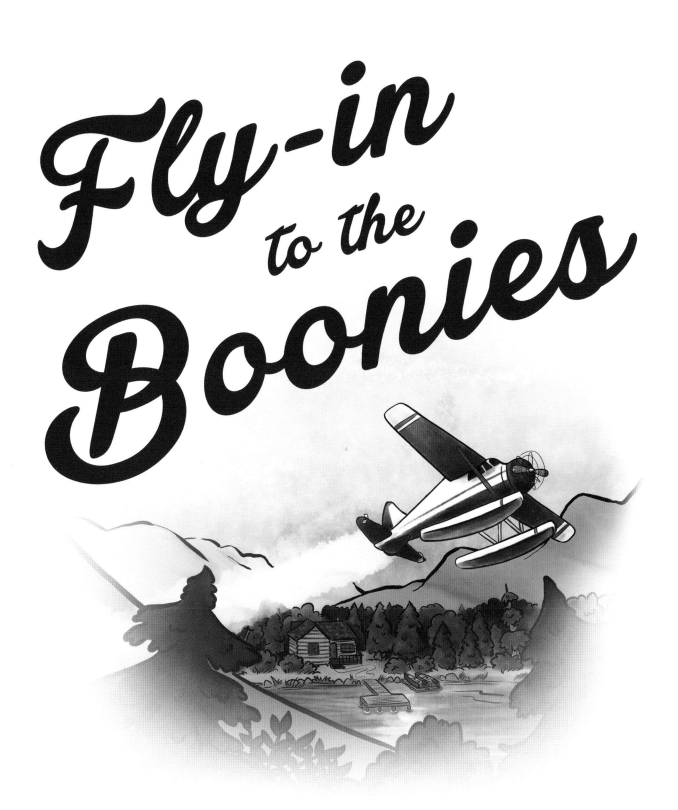

WRITTEN BY
BOB ALLEN

ILLUSTRATED BY
ERIN BOE

BEAVER'S POND
PRESS

To my fishing buddy Jim, for all the fly-in trips we have taken together, ending each day with his request, "One more cast."
—B.A.

To Camp UniStar, my own personal heaven in the Northwoods, and all the wonderful staff and volunteers that keep it running.
—E.B.

ISBN 13: 978-1-59298-606-4
Library of Congress Catalog Number: 2018912683
Printed in the United States of America
First Printing: 2019
23 22 21 20 19   5 4 3 2 1

Editor: Lily Coyle

Beaver's Pond Press
7108 Ohms Lane
Edina, MN 55439–2129
(952) 829-8818
www.BeaversPondPress.com

To order, call (800)-901-3480. Reseller discounts available.

We're headed to the boonies and we can hardly wait.
We load the plane completely and don't forget the bait.

We taxi slowly down the lake,
take our position, and turn around.

The engine roars to life and then
we're off the water, skyward bound.

We slowly climb into the wind
and barely miss a tree.

An eagle leaps out of our way
and squawks "Look out for me!"

We circle 'round while looking down
and spot a mama bear.
She's guarding cubs in nearby shrubs
so we'll stay far from there.

As we turn and dive down left
the pilot spies a moose.

Look there in the lily pads—
a moose is on the loose!

Our rustic camp is just below,
so tiny from the sky!

We glide between the rocks and trees
then splash down safe and dry

A loon is calling near our camp.
The moon is shining bright.

The campfire sparks to life and burns.
We're roasting s'mores tonight.

We snuggle in our sleeping bags,
dozing warm and cozy.

When we wake up we see our breath
and feel our cheeks turn rosy.

We grab the gear and load the boat.
It's time to wet a line.
We troll about and cruise around—

Stop here! This spot looks fine!

A nearby beaver slaps his tail
then dives down with a spray.

He pops back up to spy on us
a little ways away.

We cast our jigs into the lake.
Before mine hits the bottom,
I feel a bite first once, then twice.

I set the hook—I've got 'em!

We search along the shoreline.
All eyes are on the lookout
for open points with wide flat rocks
and space to have a cookout.

We find a spot amongst the trees
and pull the boat ashore.
We unload the grill, the pan,
some cooking stuff, and more.

We gather sticks,

Gramps starts the fire,

and Dad cleans fish
for lunch.

The fish are fried, it's time to eat.
We sit on logs and munch.

Beavers, moose, bears, and loons,

we hope to see you next year.

It's always fun to board the plane,
but we would like to stay here!

We climb out of the boonies,
so sad to say good-bye
to our heaven in the Northwoods.
Farewell, boonies, time to fly!